DISCARD
P9-DIG-109

AMIRA'S PICTURE DAY

BY REEM FARUQI

ILLUSTRATED BY FAHMIDA AZIM

HOLIDAY HOUSE • NEW YORK

Amira peered through the window, but saw only the black unblinking sky. "Do you see the moon?" whispered Mom.

R0460800838

Ziyad scanned the sky and shouted,
"I think I see it!"

"I see it too!" Amira said.

Mom drew them in for a hug. "That means it's Eid tomorrow."

Amira felt warm and tingly inside. She couldn't keep still even when she tried. She rushed to bring her mom the mehndi cone.

In a few minutes, her hands were decorated with wet green swirls
and designs. Her mom even doodled her favorite animal, a dolphin,
in the middle of one hand with a mermaid on the other.

Amira held her hands out carefully to make sure they dried.
She hoped that the next morning her mehndi designs would
be a deep chocolate brown.

"Tomorrow we get to skip school!" yelled Ziyad.
Amira cheered.

"Okay you two! Let's use your energy to make some goody bags," said Mom.

Amira joined her little brother in counting lollipops for the children at the masjid.

A colorful flyer on the fridge caught her eye. Tomorrow was
Picture Day. Amira's cheeks felt hot. Her insides felt cold.
She had already chosen her pink-striped dress.

Ms. Bailey had told them that tomorrow they would be taking a group photo of the entire 2B class.

"Mom! Tomorrow is Picture Day at school!" wailed Amira.

"Don't worry, Amira. We'll take plenty of pictures of you at the masjid in your new Eid clothes," said her mom, ironing Amira's shalwar kameez.

Amira knew it wouldn't be the same. She loved
Eid and the party at the masjid, but she didn't want
to be left out of her class picture.

How would her classmates remember her if she
wasn't there? Amira brushed her thoughts away
as she tried to fall asleep that night.

The next morning Mom woke her. "Eid Mubarak, Amira!"

Amira traced the mehndi on her hands dreamily. Her mermaid and dolphin were a deep chocolate brown!

Amira smiled as she got out of bed thinking of all the Eid treats she would get today.

Her new Eid shalwar kameez
hung nearby. Suddenly,
she spotted the pink-striped
Picture Day dress. The more
Amira thought of Picture Day,
the longer she took to
get dressed.

When Amira was finally ready, she looked in the mirror. Tiny mirrors on her blue shalwar kameez shone happily in the sunlight.

As she was leaving the room, Amira took one last look longingly at her pink-striped dress.

"Mom, are you sure it's Eid *today*, not tomorrow? Can I still go to school for Picture Day? Ms. Bailey will miss me!" pleaded Amira.

"Amira, we saw the moon. It's Eid today. Now, let's go!" answered Baba.

Seeing the masjid,
Amira's sadness
floated away.
Her mouth popped
open. She could
hardly recognize it.

Streamers with stars hung on the wall and colorful
balloons decorated the ceiling. Amira swung her basket
of goody bags proudly.

She could hardly focus on the melodious
Eid prayer—she smelled the fresh scent of
just-baked cookies. She smiled to herself
as she prayed.

Right after the Eid prayer, she rushed to her basket and handed out the goody bags to her friends at the masjid.

Lots of Mom's friends gave Amira hugs.
She made sure to hug them back and wish
them Eid Mubarak when she remembered.
It was only when her aunt Farah Khala
told Amira to smile big for a photo that
she remembered Picture Day.
Amira smiled small.

After the exciting Eid celebration at the masjid,
Amira looked around. A few balloons floated down
to the floor. She felt like one of those balloons.
If only she had not missed Picture Day.

On the way home, Amira closed her eyes tightly to hold back tears.

Suddenly, Amira had an idea. Holding her breath, she began to count her leftover goody bags quickly. There were just enough for her class!

"Mom, Baba, can we stop by my class and deliver the extra goody bags to them?"

Her parents' faces softened while they exchanged a look. "Sure, Amira," answered her mom.

"Do you think I might make it for Picture Day?" she asked.

"I'm not sure," Mom explained. "According to the flyer, 2B's photos are in the afternoon, so let's hope you're on time."

As Baba and Ziyad waited in the car,
Amira looked down at her shalwar kameez.
She wasn't wearing her pink-striped dress
for Picture Day, but she was here at school!
Feeling a little funny, she walked stiffly inside.
Each leg felt like a wobbly tower of blocks.

In classroom 2B, the class was busy getting in line. Had Amira missed Picture Day?

"Just in time, Amira!" said Ms. Bailey. "I love your outfit!"

Amira's mom explained to Ms. Bailey that today was Eid and that the family had been to the masjid to celebrate this special day for Muslims. As her teacher and mom chatted, Amira handed the basket of goody bags shyly to her teacher.

"I like your hands!" said Rafael.
"Your clothes are so colorful!" added Wei.
"You look like a princess!" gasped Reagan.
"That's what my name means," giggled Amira
as she skipped into the line.

What a perfect end to Eid! As the class stood together in the gym, the photographer told them to smile. Amira did not need to be told to smile. She was already smiling.

AUTHOR NOTE

In countries such as the United States where the majority of people are not Muslim, many Muslim children miss school on Eid. As a child, it can be fun to skip school, but what happens when Eid falls on an important day such as Picture Day? Muslims use the lunar calendar, so they do not know the exact date for Eid until they spot the new moon's crescent. This can sometimes be tricky, especially when explaining to non-Muslim teachers, classmates, coworkers, and others.

On Eid, the Muslim community comes together for a special Eid prayer at the masjid and to wish each other Eid Mubarak! Many people wear their finest clothes and are full of excitement. Children will enjoy delicious treats and receive gifts. The rest of the Eid day is usually spent having fun by visiting friends and family.

Eid prayers occur in congregation in the early morning, so Muslims are usually free to socialize in the afternoons or catch a good nap, or in Amira's situation make it to school for Picture Day! Eid Mubarak!

MORE ABOUT EID

Muslims celebrate Eid two times a year. The first Eid of the year is known as Eid al-Fitr. It occurs at the end of the month of Ramadan, the month in which Muslims fast from before sunrise to sunset. The second Eid of the year is called Eid al-Adha. It celebrates the completion of the Hajj pilgrimage. Although only pilgrims in Makkah participate in Hajj, Muslims around the world join them in celebrating Eid al-Adha.

GLOSSARY

Baba: This means father or dad in Arabic, Urdu, and other languages.

Eid Mubarak!: Have a blessed Eid!

shalwar kameez: These are traditional clothes worn in central Asia, including Pakistan and India. The kameez is a long flowy shirt. A shalwar is a pair of loose trousers that are wide at the top and skinny at the ankle. Men and women both wear shalwar and kameezes, but each style is different.

mehndi: This is the Urdu (Pakistani language) word for a fragrant paste, made from a plant, that is usually applied through a cone-shaped tube. It is used to decorate girls' and women's hands on special occasions such as Eid and weddings. The color stays on for a few days until it fades. In Arabic, mehndi is called henna.

masjid: This is a mosque or a place of worship for Muslims.

For my three brothers who always make Eid special
—Hamzah, Talha, and Osman —R. F.

For my sisters, Eid Mubarak!—F. A.

Text copyright © 2021 by Reem Faruqi
Illustrations copyright © 2021 by Fahmida Azim
All Rights Reserved
HOLIDAY HOUSE is registered in the U.S. Patent and Trademark Office.
Printed and bound in June 2021 at Leo Paper, Heshan, China.
The artwork was created with a Wacom Cintiq Pro tablet and Clip Studio Paint EX software.
www.holidayhouse.com

First Edition
3 5 7 9 10 8 6 4 2

Library of Congress Cataloging-in-Publication Data

Names: Faruqi, Reem, author. | Azim, Fahmida, illustrator.
Title: Amira's picture day / by Reem Faruqi ; illustrated by Fahmida Azim.
Description: First edition. | New York : Holiday House, [2021]
Audience: Ages 4–8. | Audience: Grades K–1. | Summary: Amira is excited because tomorrow is Eid with special clothes, treats, gifts, and a morning party at her mosque; but then she realizes that she is going to miss class picture day at school, something she was also looking forward to— so Amira has to figure out a way to be in two places at once.
Identifiers: LCCN 2020009430 | ISBN 9780823440191 (hardcover)
Subjects: LCSH: ʿĪd al-Fitr—Juvenile fiction. | Fasts and feasts—Islam—Juvenile fiction. | Islam—Customs and practices—Juvenile fiction. | Muslims—United States—Juvenile fiction. Middle Eastern Americans—Juvenile fiction. | Schools—Juvenile fiction. | CYAC: ʿĪd al-Fitr—Fiction. | Fasts and feasts—Islam—Fiction. | Islam—Customs and practices—Fiction. Muslims—United States—Fiction. | Middle Eastern Americans—Fiction. Schools—Fiction.
Classification: LCC PZ7.1.F37 Am 2021 | DDC [E]—dc23
LC record available at https://lccn.loc.gov/2020009430
ISBN: 978-0-8234-4019-1 (hardcover)